MEET THE GIRL TALK CHARACTERS

Sabrina Wells is petite, with curly auburn hair, sparkling hazel eyes, and a bubbly personality. Sabrina loves magazines, shopping, sleepovers, and most of all, she loves talking to her best friends.

Katie Campbell is a straight-A student and super athlete. With her blond hair, blue eyes, and matching clothes, she's everyone's idea of Little Miss Perfect. But Katie has a few surprises for everyone, including herself!

Randy Zak has just moved to Acorn Falls from New York City, and is she ever cool! With her radical spiked haircut and her hip New York clothes, Randy teaches everyone just how much fun it is to be different.

Allison Cloud is a Native American Indian. Allison's supersmart and really beautiful. But she has one major problem: She's thirteen years old, five foot seven, and still growing!

Girl Talk

KATIE'S CLOSE CALL

By L. E. Blair

GIRL TALK® series created by Western Publishing Company, Inc.

Western Publishing Company, Inc., Racine, Wisconsin 53404

R MCMXCIII

Text by Crystal Johnson

Chapter One

"Wow, Randy! Listen to your horoscope!" Sabrina Wells glanced up excitedly from the copy of the *Acorn Falls Gazette* she was reading. She brushed back a strand of her curly red hair and squinted at the newsprint: "'The planet Mars has moved into your sign this month,'" she read, "'bringing increased creativity and romance.' Isn't that great?"

My name is Katie Campbell. I was sitting with my three best friends, Sabrina Wells, Allison Cloud, and Randy Zak, and having lunch in the cafeteria of our school, Bradley Junior High.

"Romance?" Allison Cloud echoed, raising one eyebrow. "Who knows, Ran, maybe your stars are matched up with a boy who's sitting right in this room," she teased, waving a hand around the cafeteria, which was packed with noisy kids, as usual.

Randy Zak grimaced as she finished taking a taste of her boysenberry yogurt. "Romance I can live without," she said. "But the creativity part is cool."

Randy is not at all interested in the dating scene, which I can understand, but she is one of the most creative people I know. She's written her own music for the band she's in, Iron Wombat, and she is the coolest dresser at Bradley, where we are all in the seventh grade together. Today she had on zebra-striped leggings, a black miniskirt, and a neon orange sweater, not to mention about four different earrings. My soft yellow sweaterdress looked pretty tame in comparison, but I liked it anyway.

"What are you talking about, Randy?" Sabs asked, lowering her newspaper. Her auburn eyebrows were knit in a frown as she stared at Randy. "Nobody can live without romance!"

Sabrina is my best friend in the world, but I have to admit, she gets a bit melodramatic sometimes, especially when it comes to guys and horoscopes.

"Sabs, I thought you were supposed to be looking at the paper for current events, not reading the horoscopes," I said, putting down my half-eaten ham sandwich.

"Ugh! Don't remind me, Katie, " Sabrina said, crinkling up her nose in distaste. "Anyway, this is relevant. I mean, the positions of the planets can have a huge effect on what happens in the world."

Randy and I looked at each other and winked, but Allison said thoughtfully, "Maybe you're right, Sabs. I read an article that said there's usually a higher crime rate when there's a full moon. So maybe wars and stuff are affected by the planets, too." Al is really smart, so if she had read it, it was probably true.

"See?" Sabs said triumphantly. "Okay, so who wants me to read their horoscope next?"

"Horoscopes are really ridiculous and immature," said a familiar, obnoxious voice right next to us. "But I guess you guys need all the help you can get."

As soon as I heard the voice, I knew that it was Stacy the Great Hansen, one of my least favorite people in the world. She and her side-kick, Eva Malone, were walking by our table with their lunch trays. Stacy is not only the principal's daughter, she is also head flag girl and head of the snobbiest clique at Bradley. She thinks she's really cool, but my friends and I just think she's a pain.

"Oh, listen to Miss Sophisticated," Randy said under her breath. "Stacy is about as mature as a Barbie doll." Even though she didn't look at Stacy, I could tell Randy wanted her to hear the Barbie doll comment.

Stacy flipped her long blond hair over her shoulder and glared at Randy. "At least I don't look like a chimpanzee cut my hair," she snorted, staring at Randy's spiky black hair. Then she and Eva walked off, laughing all the way to their lunch table at the other end of the cafeteria.

"Ooh! She makes me so mad," Sabs said, stabbing her fork into the meatloaf on her tray. "How could she say that to you, Randy? I mean, I think your hair looks great."

Randy just shrugged. "Thanks, Sabs. Actually, I took it as a compliment. I figure if a jerk like Stacy doesn't like my hair, it must look pretty good. What would really worry me is if she ever starts complimenting me!"

"Stacy's never happy unless she can say

something that she thinks will bother us," Allison said.

"Yeah, I guess you guys are right," Sabs agreed, brightening. Turning back to her newspaper, she said, "I'll read your horoscope next, Katie."

My stomach was feeling kind of funny and I wasn't really hungry anyway, so I pushed my unfinished sandwich away and listened.

"Pay attention to a nagging worry . . . " Sabs began. She was holding the newspaper up in front of her, and since I was sitting directly across from her, it blocked my view of everything else in the cafeteria. I looked at it idly while she read.

Suddenly, an announcement on the back page caught my eye, and I began to read it to myself:

COACHES WANTED FOR NEW COMMUNITY
JUNIOR HOCKEY LEAGUE
AND MENTOR PROGRAM

The article went on to describe the program for underprivileged children, and it gave a meeting time and place for anyone who was interested in volunteering.

"Hold on a sec, Sabs!" I said, before she finished reading my horoscope. I reached out to hold the paper still and pointed to the article I had just read. "Look. There's a new mentor program in Acorn Falls," I began.

Sabs flipped the paper over and stared at the ad, a puzzled look on her face. "Mentor program? What's that?"

"You've heard of Big Brothers and Big Sisters, right? You know, that big national organization?" I asked.

Allison nodded, tugging thoughtfully on the end of her long braid. "They work with children from broken homes or underprivileged urban communities and match them with kind of an adopted older brother or sister. Then they have someone to do things with who can be kind of a role model for them," she said. "They don't operate anywhere near here, though."

"One of their offices is near my dad's apartment in New York City," Randy added.

"Well, this new program sounds a lot like that," I explained. "It's called the Acorn League."

Sabrina plunked the paper down and looked at me. "Wow, I think it's great that we're going to have something like that here," she said. "So, are you going to volunteer or something?"

I nodded, realizing that that was exactly what I wanted to do. "I'd like to. They're looking for coaches to help start a hockey league for underprivileged kids in the Minneapolis suburban area," I explained, feeling excited about this. "Sign-ups are Tuesday at three at the public library on Main Street. Hey, that's today."

"You're a great hockey player, Katie," Randy told me. "That sounds right up your alley."

Sabs nodded her head in agreement. "That's so cool! I wish I could play hockey, so I could help out, too," she said.

"Wait!" Al put in, leaning over to read the paper. "They also need volunteers to read to the younger kids at the library on Wednesday and Friday afternoons." She looked at Sabs and Randy, her dark eyes shining. "We could do that!"

"I'd definitely be into that," Randy said right away. I never knew she was interested in working with children, but I guess you learn new things about people all the time.

"Me, too. Let's sign up," Sabs agreed.

I grinned at my friends. I was really happy that they were psyched about helping out the Acorn League, too. "This is going to be great," I told them. "It would be more fun if you guys were coaching with me, though," I added.

"Coaching? Coaching what?" I heard Michel's voice say.

My tall stepbrother Michel was standing next to our table, and Scottie Silver was next to him. Both boys looked at me curiously. The three of us were teammates on Bradley's boys hockey team last season, so it wasn't surprising that they wanted to know what I would be coaching.

"Here, read this," I said. I handed the *Gazette* over to Michel and Scottie and pointed to the ad for the Acorn League. I wasn't sure if they would want to volunteer, too. I mean, maybe boys wouldn't be interested in working with little kids. I really hoped they'd be into it, though. Then the teams would have more coaches and I would have some friends with me.

Randy must have had the same thought,

because she punched Michel lightly on the arm and said, "It's perfect! You guys have to join. You're two of the best skaters in the school — besides Katie, of course."

"Thanks a lot," Scottie said sarcastically, but his blue eyes were twinkling as he looked down at me. I tried hard not to blush. Scottie and I aren't boyfriend and girlfriend or anything, but I guess we kind of like each other.

"*Très bien*. It sounds great!" Michel exclaimed after he read the ad. "We will join with you, K.C. Eh, Scottie?" Michel is French-Canadian, but we've all gotten used to his accent since he moved to Acorn Falls.

Scottie nodded. "Sure. It will help keep us in shape during the off-season," he agreed.

"Great!" I cried.

"K.C., are you going to eat those cookies?" Michel asked, eyeing the plastic bag of oatmeal cookies that sat next to my unfinished sandwich. They were usually my favorite cookies and our cook makes them really thick and chewy, but today I just couldn't eat them.

I sat up a little straighter in my chair, hoping my stomachache would go away soon. "No, go ahead," I said, pushing the cookies toward Michel.

He shoved a whole cookie in his mouth and offered one to Scottie, who did the same. The two of them stood there and gobbled up the whole bag in under a minute. Sometimes guys can be so gross!

Just then the bell rang, signaling the end of the lunch period. My friends and I began to gather up our books and throw out our garbage.

"Let's all meet by Sabs's and my locker after last class and walk over to the library together," I suggested to everyone before we went to our different classes.

"Wait, what about Mrs. Smith?" Michel reminded me.

"I'll call her and ask if she'll pick us up later at the library and drive us home," I told him.

Ever since Michel's father married my mother and we moved to the outskirts of town, our housekeeper or my older sister Emily has to drive us to and from school every day. It's a pain sometimes, but I guess I really shouldn't mind too much. It is nice living in our new house, which has an indoor pool, tennis courts, a pond, and even stables.

Sometimes I feel guilty that we have so much when some people have so little. But now I could volunteer to help children who weren't as lucky as I was. It made me feel good to think that helping out with the Acorn League might give kids opportunities that they wouldn't have otherwise.

As I walked to class, I wondered what the kids in the program would be like. I couldn't wait to find out!

Chapter Two

"I am very happy to see such a good turnout today," said the tall, striking black woman who stood in front of the group of people assembled at the library. She had big brown eyes and smooth cocoa-colored skin. She was wearing a gray-and-ivory checkered skirt with an ivory sweater.

The woman had just introduced herself as Mrs. Walker, telling us that she was in charge of the Acorn League. Then she told us about the history of the Acorn League. She seemed really dedicated and enthusiastic about the entire program.

Sabrina, Randy, Michel, Allison, Scottie, and I sat at one of the library's round wooden tables while we listened. I was glad to see that the other tables were almost full as well. There were other junior high school kids there, but most of the volunteers were older. There were several women who looked about the same age as my mom, and even some senior citizens. I figured that they must be there to join the reading program, since they didn't exactly look like hockey types.

"The hockey group and the reading group will meet for one hour every Wednesday and Friday at three-thirty," Mrs. Walker was saying now. "I will pick the children up in our mini van and bring them over right after school. We ask that you all arrive promptly since we only have the children for two hours a week."

Mrs. Walker gazed expectantly around the room. "Just so I can get an idea, how many of you are here to coach the hockey league for children ages seven to nine?" she asked.

Michel, Scottie, and I raised our hands. Looking around, I saw that I was right — the only other people to raise their hands were two of the high school boys. Everyone else was there for the reading program.

Mrs. Walker didn't seem to mind at all, though. "Good!" she said enthusiastically. "That should be plenty to get two teams off the ground. Now, I warn you. Many of the children you will be coaching are novices at skating. In fact, most have never owned their own skates."

I exchanged a worried look with Michel and Scottie. This was going to be harder than I had thought if these kids didn't even know how to skate!

"But we were lucky enough to get skates through community donations," Mrs. Walker continued. "And Bradley Junior High has generously offered to let us use their hockey rink for two hours a week. That is where you will be meeting tomorrow for your first practice. The reading program will take place right here, in the Children's Room of the library."

Mrs. Walker held up a sheet of lined looseleaf paper. "Now, if everyone will sign their name and write their phone number on this sheet, we can go into the Children's Room and meet the kids you'll be working with."

I looked over to the right, where a door was marked CHILDREN'S ROOM. Through the glass, I saw a group of little kids playing.

"Wow, we get to meet the kids now!" Sabs said excitedly as we waited for the sign-up sheet to reach our table. "I can't wait. I love little kids. I want to have at least ten kids when I grow up!"

"Ten!" Randy, Al, and I cried in unison.

"*Mon Dieu*, Sabrina. You better tell whomever you're going to marry *that* before the wedding!" Michel said, breaking into laughter.

Sabs kind of has a crush on Michel, so of course she blushed. "You mean you don't like kids?" she asked.

"Sure, but ten?" Michel shook his head.

Scottie jabbed Michel in the side and said, "Just think, then you could have enough people for your own hockey team!"

The sign-up sheet reached our table right at that moment, so Sabs snatched it up and wrote her name down. She seemed really glad to stop that conversation!

Once we had all signed up, we made our way to the Children's Room. It was separated from the main part of the library by glass doors so the kids could make all the noise they wanted without disturbing everyone else. Boy, was it noisy in there! Kids were all over the place, eating cookies and drinking milk and running around.

I hesitated just inside the door, not sure where to begin. I should have known that Sabs wouldn't be at all intimidated by this situation, though. The minute she stepped through the glass doors, she went over to a group of kids who were sitting and eating cookies. "Aren't they adorable?" she cooed.

Before I knew it, Sabs was talking to a cute little redheaded girl who was wearing a striped dress that looked a little too big for her. Randy and Al went over to a different group of kids and helped pour some milk for them.

Many of the kids looked too young to play hockey, so I tried to find some that looked a little older. Mrs. Walker said they had to be at least seven years old.

Michel and Scottie had stopped just inside the doors, too, I noticed. They were both leaning against the wall with their hands stuffed in their pockets, looking totally confused. I guess they weren't sure how to act around little kids.

"Come on, you guys," I told them. "Let's try and figure out who's going to be playing hockey."

"How are we going to get them to slow down enough to talk to us?" Michel asked, eyeing a group of boys who were running around the low table in the center of the room.

Scottie opened his mouth to say something, but then he was suddenly pushed from behind.

"Hey, cut that out!" he said, grabbing a little boy who had just shoved another child. Scottie looked back at Michel and me. "Did you see that? This kid just pushed that little girl!"

As Scottie bent down to make sure the girl was okay, I looked closely at the boy who had pushed her. I guessed that he was about seven or eight years old. He had dark wavy hair and big brown eyes. And he was glaring at Scottie.

Oh, great, I thought. Our first hockey player, and he's a troublemaker! Then I reminded myself that the whole reason we were here was to help these kids out. I figured that I should at least get to know this kid before I started judging him.

I went over to the boy and squatted down so I was eye-level with him. I had forgotten all about my stomachache, but now I winced a little as my abdomen got squashed.

"Hi," I said to the little boy, pushing

thoughts of my stomach out of my mind. "What's your name?"

The little boy frowned at me. "Danny," he answered me curtly. Then he crossed his arms stubbornly over his chest and looked away.

"My name's Katie. You know, Danny, it's not so nice to push other kids around like that," I told him.

Danny rolled his eyes up toward the ceiling, as if he'd heard that line before. Obviously he didn't care whether it was nice or not. "How old are you?" I asked, changing the subject.

"Eight," he answered, still not looking at me. This little kid wasn't making it very easy to be his mentor, that was for sure!

I tried to think of something to say that would catch Danny's interest. "Well, if you're eight, that means that you'll be in the hockey program with me!" I told him, trying to sound as enthusiastic as possible.

Danny just shrugged. "Big deal," he said.

He was starting to make me mad, but I was determined to get through to this kid. "Do you know how to skate?" I asked.

At first he didn't answer me, but after a

few minutes of silence, he finally replied, "I used to, but I'm too old for that now."

Too old? How could someone who was only eight be too old for anything? "Well, it's not something you forget. A little practice and you'll be flying on the ice like a pro," I told him, hoping that would get him interested in this hockey program.

"I don't know why my mom is making me do this anyway! It's stupid!" Danny suddenly burst out. He finally looked at me then, and his brown eyes were flashing with anger. "I'd rather just hang out with my friends after school at the park like I usually do."

I looked at Danny in surprise. He was only eight years old, and he usually hung out in the park? When I was his age, I wasn't even allowed to go to the park without my parents or at least Emily.

I knew that Danny and some of the other children present came from a town called Hadley. It was about twenty minutes away from Acorn Falls, closer to Minneapolis, and I had heard stories on the local news about over-crowded apartment buildings and serious crime. It didn't seem safe for a young boy to be out on the streets alone!

I couldn't help asking, "Your parents let you go to the park by yourself?"

"My mom doesn't care. She doesn't even know. She works until dark every night. My dad isn't around," he told me quickly.

For the first time I realized exactly how important this program was. Somebody had to get kids like Danny off the streets. Otherwise, they might be influenced by bad older kids, or maybe even hurt.

"Danny, listen to me," I said, holding his shoulders so that he had to face me directly. "First of all, I'm sure your mom cares about you a lot. She just probably works really hard since your dad isn't around. And sometimes when grown-ups work hard and get tired, they don't have as much time to spend with you as they should."

Danny didn't look convinced, but at least he was listening to me.

"And second," I continued, "we're going to have a lot of fun. I'll teach you how to skate better than anyone you know. And when our team plays other teams, it'll be really exciting. It doesn't even matter if we win or lose — you still feel great because you know you did your best!" I ruffled his hair, trying to win him over. "So, can I count on you to come every time and try your hardest?" I asked hopefully.

Danny gave me a really hard, probing look. I had the feeling that he was trying to decide whether to trust me or not. Finally, the look in his eyes softened, and he nodded his head slowly.

"Great!" I said, grinning at him.

Just then another boy walked up to us. Immediately Danny's face took on its tough look again. "I mean, I don't really have any choice except to play on the dumb team," he said gruffly. Then he stalked off, with the other boy following him.

This definitely wasn't going to be easy, I thought as I watched the two boys start wrestling. But I was pretty sure that I had started to break down Danny's defenses, and that made me feel really good.

Maybe I could make a difference. Even if I helped just one little boy, it would be worth it!

Chapter Three

"Will somebody help me with my skates?" a little girl's tiny voice asked.

It was after school on Wednesday, and I had just walked into Bradley Junior High's skating rink with Michel and Scottie. Looking in the direction the voice had come from, I saw a girl with copper-colored hair sitting on the bench next to the rink. She was struggling to lace up her skates.

"Sure," I said, smiling at the little girl. I remembered her from the day before, and that her name was Joanna. I knelt down next to her, while Michel and Scottie went to help other kids who were scattered around the benches next to the rink.

As I worked to untangle a knot in Joanna's laces, I noticed that her skates were old and worn and the laces were frayed. I knew we were lucky to get these donations at all, but still, I decided that I would look around our storage room at home to see if I had saved any of my old skates. I didn't know whether or not Mom had gotten rid of them when we moved into the new house, but if I still had a pair, I wanted to donate them to the Acorn League.

"Okay, everyone!" Mrs. Walker clapped her hands to get our attention just as I finished showing Joanna how to lace up her skates tightly, to give her ankles the most support. The rest of the kids were all over the place, so I helped Michel, Scottie, and the other two coaches steer them over to sit on the bleachers. Finally, everyone quieted down.

First Mrs. Walker told us that she would stay with us for the first class but that after that the kids would be under our supervision, along with coach Budd, the hockey coach. Then she explained how the hockey program would work.

"We will divide the children into two teams. The coaches will have a few days to teach everyone the basic skills and rules of the game. Then, a week from Friday, we will have our first scrimmage between the two teams." Mrs. Walker smiled broadly as she added, "We will invite the children's parents, if they can make it, to show them what progress you've all made."

"A week from Friday!" I whispered under my breath. That didn't seem like nearly enough time to get together a team. We didn't even know if these kids could skate!

I thought I had whispered, but I guess Mrs. Walker heard me. She looked at me and said, "Yes, I know, it's not a lot of time. But I really want the parents to be involved right from the start. Of course, no one will expect a perfect team at the very beginning. But I'm sure parents will be eager to see their children's progress, so I will be inviting them back every month or so. Now, if there aren't any questions, I'll let you get started."

Michel and Scottie hurried over to me as soon as Mrs. Walker stopped talking.

"*Mon Dieu!* We better get working right away," Michel exclaimed. "We have to have a winning team in less than two weeks!" He grabbed a hockey stick for himself from a pile next to the ice.

The other two coaches came over to where all the equipment was piled up, so we finally had a chance to meet them. Their names were John and Dave, and they were both on the high school hockey team. Scottie knew them a little from going to Bradley High games.

"Um, where should we start?" Michel wanted to know. He looked over at the kids, who were all looking at us expectantly. I noticed that Danny was sitting a little apart from the other kids, as if he were too cool for them.

"We'd better explain the equipment and stuff first," I suggested.

"Definitely," said Dave. "We can't assume that they know anything, so we better start with the very basics."

The five of us went over to the kids and showed them how to put the safety pads on their knees and elbows, and how to wear the protective masks.

Next we lined everyone up on the ice and handed out hockey sticks. Let me tell you, it took a lot of energy to show them how to use the sticks safely, without smacking each other! I was glad to have something to keep me busy, though, because it kept my mind off my stomach. It was still hurting me, but I wasn't about to let it interfere with coaching these kids.

"Now what?" John asked as he and Dave skated over to Scottie, Michel, and me.

Scottie glanced at the line of eager children. "Why don't we just let everyone skate around for a while?" he said. "Then we can see how good everyone is. We want to make sure the two teams are pretty evenly matched, right?"

We all agreed that that was a good idea. The kids were definitely happy to begin actually skating, even though we made them skate without their hockey sticks at first. I was happy to see that all of them could at least skate, but some kids were better than others.

Even though I kept an eye on all the kids, I have to admit that I watched Danny the most. He pretended to have a bored expression on his face, but I could see the excited glimmer in his eyes. It was obvious that he really did love to skate. He was already whizzing around the rink, passing other kids who weren't as good.

"I think Danny would make a pretty good center," I told the other coaches, pointing him out. He was fast and agile, which are definitely good things to be when you're a center. The other guys all agreed with me.

Then Michel pointed out two kids, Joanna and a little boy, who obviously didn't have much skating experience. We decided to make them goalies, since it wasn't so important to be a strong skater for that position.

Trying to figure out which position would be best for each child was really challenging. A hockey team includes a center, who is at the center of the skating field, and the left wing and the right wing positions. We picked the fastest skaters for those positions. In addition to the center and the left and right wings, there are also two defensive players who protect the goalie. For those positions we tried to find bigger players who might have an easier time blocking. And of course, there's the goalie, making six players in all. We counted twelve children skating around, so there were enough for two teams.

We divided the kids into the teams. Michel, Scottie, and I decided to coach one team, and Dave and John took the other one. I made sure we got the team with Danny on it, but both teams had good skaters and bad skaters.

"All right!" Michel exclaimed after the teams were set. "This is working out *très bien*."

We had only about fifteen minutes left now, so we decided to let the kids keep skating around however they wanted. We handed out the hockey sticks again and put some pucks on the ice so they could get used to hitting them around.

"Hey, Danny. You're pretty good!" I said, skating over to him after he hit a puck past another little boy and into one of the goal nets.

He looked up at me, his cheeks red from skating. I couldn't believe it, but he actually smiled at me. This hockey league definitely seemed to be having a good effect on him.

But then Danny gave me a critical look. "How come you play hockey?" he asked. "You're a girl."

"She may be a girl, but she's also the best left wing on the Bradley Junior High team," Scottie said, skating over to Danny and me.

Danny looked at me dubiously. "Really?" he asked.

"Yeah," Scottie told him. Then he looked kind of embarrassed that he had complimented me. "But we all know that the very best hockey position is the center," he added, patting Danny on the back.

Of course, that made Danny really happy, since we had just told him that his position on the team was center. Still, I wasn't going to let Scottie get away with bragging like that. "Hey, just because you play center on our team doesn't mean that's a better position than a wing, Scottie Silver!" I said defensively.

Scottie grinned at me, his blue eyes crinkling in the corners. "So I'm a little prejudiced!"

I laughed. "Well, you better not try to —"

Suddenly my dull stomachache turned into a sharp stabbing pain in my right side, and I doubled over.

"Katie, what's wrong?" Scottie cried, bending over and holding me up with one arm.

After what seemed like forever, the pain started to fade and I could breathe again. "I'm fine," I said, even though I really felt pretty awful.

"Fine?" he echoed, frowning at me. "Then why can't you even stand up straight?" he asked, still holding me up with his arm.

I gritted my teeth and forced myself to straighten up, trying not to show that my stomach still hurt. "There, I'm fine," I said again.

"Katie!" Scottie said knowingly. I'm not a very good liar, and I guess Scottie could see right through me.

"It's nothing, Scottie, I swear. I just have a stomach virus or a cramp or something, that's all," I told him.

I hoped that what I'd said was true, but deep down I was beginning to get worried. I had never had a stomachache for two whole days, especially one that would suddenly hurt so badly.

"What's up?" Michel asked, skating to a stop next to us. "What are you two talking so seriously about?"

"Nothing!" I said quickly. "I just had a cramp or something."

Before Michel or Scottie could say anything, I skated away. I tried to breathe normally, but no matter how hard I tried, I couldn't quite block out the pain in my stomach.

Somehow I managed to make it through the rest of the hour until practice was finally over and Mrs. Walker got all the kids back on the bus that would take them back to Hadley. I was really relieved when Michel, Scottie, and I could stop skating and take off our own skates.

All I wanted to do was go home and crawl into bed, but I couldn't. We had agreed to meet Sabs, Randy, and Al at Fitzie's Soda Shoppe after their reading session at the library with the Acorn League's younger kids.

"Hey, guys, slow down," I cried as Scottie and Michel walked quickly ahead of me down Main Street. I held one hand on my stomach and tried to catch up, but running made my stomach hurt more and my head feel dizzy.

"Come on, K.C. Are you out of shape already? Hockey season ended only a little while ago," Michel teased as he and Scottie turned and waited for me.

When I caught up to them, Scottie gave me this probing look. "That cramp again?" he asked.

"Yeah," I mumbled, without looking him in the eye.

Scottie reached over and took my skates from me. "I'll carry those."

Normally I would have told him that I could carry my own hockey skates, but today I didn't feel like it. I got a sudden chill and pulled my coat closer around me. "Thanks," I said softly.

"Come on," Michel said, pulling on my sleeve. "I'm hungry!"

Luckily, Fitzie's is only a few blocks from Bradley and we were there in about five minutes. I was glad to get inside where it was warm. I couldn't stop shaking because I was so cold.

The second we walked into Fitzie's I spotted Sabs. Her curly red hair is hard to miss! She and Randy and Al had gotten a big booth in the back. Fitzie's wasn't too crowded, which wasn't surprising since it was already a quarter to five. Most of the kids who came here after school had already left.

"I'm going to have a burger and fries," Michel announced even before he had his down coat off.

When the waitress walked over, everyone ordered stuff like fries, soda, hamburgers, and ice cream. But when it was my turn to order, I just said, "I'll have a cup of tea, please." I remembered that my grandmother used to say that herbal tea would help a stomachache. I knew Fitzie's didn't have herbal tea, but I thought maybe the regular kind would work just as well.

"Tea?" Sabs repeated. "Don't you want fries or anything?"

I shook my head. "I'm not hungry."

"So how did hockey practice go today?" Al asked us. I was really relieved that she changed the subject.

"Great! Those little kids are pretty good." Michel spoke up right away.

"We even have a scrimmage a week from next Friday with parents coming," Scottie added, picking up a menu and looking at it.

Randy had grabbed two forks and was drumming them on the table. "That doesn't sound like a lot of time to teach them how to play hockey," she commented.

"Hey, maybe we can ask Mrs. Walker if we can bring our reading group to the game!" Sabrina suggested, looking at Randy and Allison.

"Sounds good to me," Randy agreed. "I definitely want to see those kids play."

Al nodded eagerly. "And then maybe we can have them talk about it in the next reading session. You know, like a show-and-tell thing," she suggested.

I just sat there feeling sick while my friends started talking about how their reading group had gone. I felt bad that I wasn't being more enthusiastic about it, but I just couldn't get into the conversation.

I happened to look up just as the waitress brought over a tray with our food. My stomach did a flip-flop when I saw all those burgers and fries and stuff, and I suddenly felt as if I was about to be sick.

"Excuse me," I cried, jumping up from the table. Everyone at the table was looking at me strangely, but I just ran to the bathroom without stopping to explain.

Luckily the queasy feeling went away a little as soon as I got away from all that greasy-looking food. Bending over the sink, I splashed some cold water on my face. That helped some, but the stabbing pain was still in my right side.

I had no idea what kind of stomachache this was, but it was different from any I had ever had before. With a sigh I leaned against the sink, stared at my pale face in the mirror, and asked, "What is wrong with me?"

Chapter Four

"What are you going to bring for tomorrow night, Katie?"

"Huh?" I asked, turning to Sabs. She, Randy, and Al were all standing next to the locker that Sabs and I share, but I hadn't really been paying attention to what they were talking about.

Al gave me a funny look as she shifted her books from one arm to the other. "We were wondering what you're going to bring to Sabs's slumber party tomorrow night," she explained. "I'm bringing popcorn, and Randy's bringing pizza."

"And I'm going to make brownies," Sabs finished. "Weren't you listening, Katie? We just went over all this."

"Sorry, guys," I said, feeling guilty. Sabs had been planning this sleepover for more than a week now, and I had totally forgotten about it!

I wasn't even sure I would be able to go if I didn't start feeling better.

Here it was, Friday morning, and I still had a stomachache. Sometimes it was dull, and sometimes it was sharp, but it had been there for over three days now. I was getting really worried.

I hadn't told anyone yet. I mean, I didn't want to get everyone anxious if it was just some stomach bug that would go away soon. But I didn't know how much longer I could hide it. Last night Mom had asked me if I was on a diet or something, because I was hardly eating anything at dinner.

I tried to think of something to take for the sleepover, but I was so preoccupied with my stomach that I couldn't think of a single thing. "What do you want me to bring?" I finally asked.

"How about soda?" Randy suggested.

"Definitely! Get diet," Sabs instructed. Sabrina always watches her weight even though she doesn't need to.

"Yuck," Randy said. "Diet soda is gross."

"I'll get one diet and one regular," I decided, just to get the issue settled.

As I reached up to get my books for my first class, out of the corner of my eye I saw Arizonna walking up behind Al and Randy. He's this really nice guy who moved here from California this year. The minute I saw him, I burst out laughing, but it made my side hurt so I tried to stop.

"Hey, dudettes! What's up?" Arizonna greeted us. He was wearing ripped jeans with fluorescent orange long johns peeking through. His blond hair was hidden under a neon green baseball cap, and he had on an extralarge bright yellow sweatshirt.

Actually, I wasn't laughing at his clothes — Arizonna dresses like that every day, and I'm used to it by now. The funny part was that he was carrying a surfboard!

"What are you doing with that?" Sabs asked, giggling as she nodded at the surf-board.

Arizonna shrugged. "We have to do an oral report on exercise for health class, so I'm doing a surfing demonstration to show that it's a good workout," he explained.

Randy elbowed Arizonna in the side. "Where do you think you're going to surf in

Minnesota? In the snow?" she kidded him.

"Very funny," he said good-naturedly. "It's just a classroom demonstration, Randy. I'm not going to really surf."

Just then the warning bell rang. "We better get going," Allison said. Turning to Randy and Sabs, she reminded them, "We're all going to walk to the library together after school for the reading group, right?"

Randy and Sabs nodded.

Arizonna's pale blue eyes lit up with interest. "Yeah, I heard about this Acorn League thing," he said, leaning his surfboard against the lockers and brushing his blond bangs out of his eyes. "How do you join?"

I wasn't surprised that he was interested in the Acorn League. Arizonna is really into things like community service and saving the environment.

"Just come with us after school," Sabs said. "I'm sure they could use more volunteers."

Sabs, Al, and Randy were going in the same direction as Arizonna, so they all walked down the hall together.

"See you in homeroom, guys," I said, starting off in the other direction.

The day went by in a total blur, probably because my stomach hurt so much that I could hardly pay attention in my classes. Ms. Staats even accused me of daydreaming in English class, which kind of upset me, since English is my favorite class and I really like Ms. Staats.

By the time school was over for the day I felt worse than ever. I was sweating and shivering at the same time, and I was feeling a little dizzy again. I knew I should probably skip the Acorn League's hockey practice that day, but I just couldn't do it. There were only two more practices before our first scrimmage, and I felt as if our team really needed my help if they were going to be ready.

When I reached my locker, I grabbed the two pairs of old skates that I had found in our basement, then went to the rink. Michel, Scottie, Dave, and John were already there with their skates on when I arrived.

"Hey, nice skates," Dave commented as I put my old skates down on one of the benches. "I think Joanna could use one of those pairs. Hers are pretty worn out."

While I put on my own skates, he called Joanna over and had her try on a pair. They fit pretty well. Another girl, Tanya, fit into the other pair. Within a few minutes, they both had on their new skates and we were ready for business.

First we put all the kids in two lines and did some passing drills. It took the kids a little while to learn how to control the puck, but after half an hour or so they sort of got the hang of it.

"What do you say, guys?" Scottie said to me and Michel at the end of one drill. "I think these kids are ready for a practice scrimmage."

"Definitely," Michel agreed. "They need to get used to their positions. And playing will be the best way for them to learn the rules of the game."

Dave and John thought a practice scrimmage would be a good idea, too, so we immediately showed the kids their positions. While John explained the basic rules, I skated over to the bench to tighten my laces. As I bent over, another jabbing pain shot through my stomach. Of course, Michel and Scottie chose that exact moment to skate over to me.

"Hey, K.C. We think that the coaches should play in the first scrimmage while some of the kids sit out and watch, just to let them see how a real game works," Michel said. Luckily he didn't seem to notice that I wasn't feeling too well. "Then after that we can have the kids join us, and then they can play by themselves."

I nodded, looking down at my skate laces so I wouldn't have to face the guys. When I straightened up I noticed that Scottie was looking at me closely, but I pretended that nothing was wrong. I hoped he wouldn't notice that I had to use a little extra effort to get myself off the bench.

"I'll play center, Michel will play goalie, and you'll be left wing, okay?" Scottie told me, still looking at me suspiciously.

"Fine," I said. I glanced down at the pile of hockey sticks on the ground and wondered how I was going to bend over to get one without crying out in pain. "Scottie, could you hand me a stick?" I asked, trying to act casually.

"Sure." He took two from the pile and handed me one, keeping the other for himself.

"Thanks," I said, then skated onto the ice.

John had finished explaining the rules to

the two teams, and he and Dave were already in position, getting ready to play right wing and center on the other team. The five kids we had replaced were sitting on the benches to watch the demonstration scrimmage. I noticed that Danny didn't look too happy to be sitting out while Scottie played his position.

Joanna, who played goalie on our team, was voted to blow the whistle for the face-off, since Michel was playing her position for now.

As soon as the whistle sounded, Scottie and Dave battled for the puck in the center of the ice. After a short scuffle, Scottie got possession of the puck, but Dave wasn't about to let him keep it. He and John surrounded Scottie, showing Michael, the little boy who was their other forward, how to do the same. I had to admit, Michael was doing a pretty good job!

Scottie looked desperately for someone to pass to. I should have been right next to him, but with the pain in my stomach, I wasn't skating as fast as usual. And Paulie, our right wing, just wasn't fast enough yet. John poked at the puck and got it away from Scottie, then passed it to Dave along the boards. Dave whizzed back past me and right through our two young and inexperienced defense players. He took a shot at the goal from head on. Michel had no chance of blocking the shot as it flew over his shoulder and into the net.

Of course, all of the kids on Dave and John's team cheered like crazy then. I felt terrible when I saw the disappointed looks on the faces of the kids on our team. Danny was actually scowling at Scottie from the bench.

I skated back to my position, feeling pretty low that I hadn't done my best to help stop the other team from scoring. I should have been there when Scottie needed me! How was I going to teach these kids to play well if I kept blowing it myself?

This time I stood poised, stick in hand, and when the second face-off came, I was ready. I was right up next to Scottie in an instant. When Dave got the puck, I whizzed up, surprised him, and stole it. I passed it up the ice to Scottie, who skillfully dodged John and the other team's two defensive players. He flew right back toward the net, which was manned by a little blond boy named Mark. I saw Scottie pause and shoot for the net a lot softer than normally. I'm sure he wanted to make sure that

Mark wouldn't get hurt with a high shot.

The puck slid easily into the net between Mark's legs. He looked upset, but Dave and John hurried over and told him he did a really good job. They took a minute to show him how to drop down on his knees to block low shots like that.

We decided that leaving the scrimmage a tie would be the best bet, so neither team would feel bad about losing. Then it was time for us coaches to sit down and watch the kids play.

I plopped down gladly on the bench, out of breath and sweaty from just those few minutes of hard skating. Whatever stomach thing I had was sure taking its toll on my hockey game.

Danny paused next to me while he and the other kids who had sat out took their positions. "You did pretty good," he told me.

That made me feel good in spite of my stomach. "Thanks!" I said. My face felt really hot all of a sudden, so I grabbed a plastic water bottle from the bench and drank thirstily.

"Are you ready for the scrimmage next Friday?" I asked Danny, putting the bottle back down.

Danny made a face. "I guess," he said. "It doesn't matter. My mom can't come. She has to work. Anyway, she doesn't care."

I hated to see him looking so disappointed and angry. "Oh, Danny. I'm sure she really wants to be there, but just can't," I explained. "Besides, I'm sure she'll be proud of you anyway."

"I guess," Danny said, frowning. He didn't look as if he completely believed me.

"Well, I'll be here cheering for you and the team, so don't be so gloomy. Come on, get out there and practice!" I said, nudging him a little.

Danny brightened a little as he scooted off onto the ice. I leaned back and took a slow breath. Being a coach for these kids definitely involved more than just teaching them hockey, but I was really loving every minute. I couldn't wait to see how they did next Friday. I just hoped by then I would be feeling better!

Chapter Five

"Katie, it's time for brunch!" I heard Michel call through my bedroom door Saturday morning.

I opened my mouth to tell him I wasn't hungry, but all that came out was a groan. A moment later, my door opened and Michel stuck his head in.

"It's eleven o'clock! Are you okay? What are you doing still in bed?"

I struggled to sit up, but the pain in my stomach made me wince. Suddenly I was really sick and tired of having this stomach problem. I just wished it would go away and that everyone would leave me alone. "I'm fine!" I snapped. "Now get out of my room!"

Michel looked surprised, then angry at my outburst. "Okay, be that way!" he yelled back. "That's the last time I come and get you for brunch!" He slammed my door shut, and I heard him stomp off down the hall.

For a second I just sat there in bed, propped up against my pillow. Then I began to cry, the hot tears spilling down my cheeks. What was wrong with me? It had been four days now, and instead of getting better, I was getting worse!

Last night I had been up until almost three in the morning, lying in bed and worrying. When I finally did fall asleep, I had nightmares about when Mom and Emily and I had gone to the hospital the night that Dad had had his heart attack and died. That had been over three years ago. I hadn't had that nightmare in a long time, but now it was back. I guess I was more worried about this stomachache than I had realized!

I still hadn't told my mom about being sick. I knew she would make me go to the doctor, which I definitely did not want to do. Seeing a doctor just reminds me of all the doctors that were around when Dad died. I guess back then, when I was younger, I kind of blamed them for not being able to save him. I know now that there was nothing they could do — heart disease runs in all the men in my father's family. There was nothing Dad or any of us could have done to avoid his getting sick.

I wiped the tears from my eyes, trying to convince myself that this was a totally different situation. What happened to my dad was definitely not going to happen to me. Taking a deep breath, I tried to think rationally about what was going on here.

My stomach had started to hurt last Tuesday. Sure, it was pretty painful, but four days wasn't really such a long time. I mean, it usually took a week for colds to go away. This thing would probably go away by itself in another day or two.

Getting together all my courage, I made a decision: If my stomach didn't feel better after a week, by next Wednesday, I would tell Mom and go to the doctor.

Deciding that made me feel a lot better. I got slowly out of bed and went into the bathroom that Michel and I share. My stomach was still hurting while I took a shower, but by the time I got dressed, the pain had gone down to a dull throb.

Glancing at the clock on my night table, I saw that it was almost noon. I had probably missed brunch by now, but I really wasn't hungry anyway. Besides, we would have lots to eat at Sabs's house later that afternoon.

I was about to go down to the kitchen to make myself some tea when the phone next to my bed rang. It was the private line that Michel and I share, so I knew it was probably Sabs calling me. I picked up the receiver and said, "Hello?"

"Hi, Katie!" Sabs's voice came over the line. "What are you doing?"

"I just got dressed," I told her.

"So late?" Sabs sounded surprised, but luckily for me she changed the subject right away. "What are you wearing? I have no idea what I should put on for tonight!"

I couldn't help laughing. "Sabs, it's only a slumber party."

"That doesn't matter. It's still important to dress right for every occasion," Sabs told me. "So what are you going to wear?" she asked again.

Glancing in the full-length mirror on the back of my door, I said, "Okay, I'm wearing my baggy jeans with a white turtleneck and my big white fisherman's sweater. Oh, and my brown boots." I didn't tell her I was wearing my baggy jeans because my stomach hurt too much to wear anything tight.

"Oh, I was thinking about wearing jeans and boots too," Sabs said, sounding disappointed.

"Sabs, it doesn't really matter!" I exclaimed.

As soon as I said that, I felt really bad. I mean, usually I love talking to Sabs about clothes and stuff, but worrying about my stomach was making me so cranky! Quickly I added, "Because we'll be inside your house the whole night, and we'll all have our shoes off anyway. Besides, I think it will be fun if we dress the same, since we're best friends and everything."

"Yeah, okay!" Sabs said. I was glad that she didn't sound mad at me or anything. "So what time will you be here? Let's make it kind of early so we can walk to the video store before dinner and pick out the movies together."

The thought of walking anywhere made me cringe. "Um, it's kind of cold out, Sabs. How about if I ask Mrs. Smith to drive us all over to the video store when she drops me off?" I suggested.

"Are you sure?" Sabrina's voice sounded doubtful. "I mean, you're always saying about how you miss being able to walk places since Mrs. Smith takes you everywhere now."

Now I had really done it. Sabs knows how I love walking no matter how cold it is outside. But I didn't want her to worry about me, so I just laughed uneasily and said, "I guess I'm getting used to having rides."

I really didn't want to keep talking about this, so I quickly added, "I'll be over at your house about four o'clock, okay?"

"Great! We'll be ready to go to the video store so Mrs. Smith doesn't have to wait for us or anything. See you then."

"Okay. Bye," I said, then hung up.

My stomach seemed to get a little worse when I went downstairs to make myself a cup of tea. I couldn't even stand the thought of going back up all those stairs to my room on the third floor, so I took my tea into the family room and sat there flipping through some magazines. I don't usually sit around inside on the weekends, but today I didn't think I could do anything else.

Finally I got up the courage to go back up

to my room. Those stairs were really hard on my stomach again. After that, I mostly just stayed in my room until it was time to go to Sabrina's. At least I didn't have to lie to anyone about being sick. Mom and Jean-Paul had gone to some kind of luncheon at the Acorn Falls Country Club, so I just saw them for two seconds when they were on their way out. Michel totally ignored me, since he was still mad, and Emily was spending the afternoon at a high school basketball game with her boyfriend Reed. No one seemed to notice that I was sick at all.

Until I got to Sabrina's house, that is. I should have known that I couldn't hide things from my friends for long. They just know me too well.

Actually, I made it through picking out the video okay. Sabs and Al and Randy were so busy deciding on what movies to watch that they didn't really pay attention to me. Then we went back to the Wellses' and started to dig into the pizza Randy had brought, which we reheated in the oven.

"How's the reading program going, you guys?" I asked when we were all sitting down at the Wellses' kitchen table. I hardly knew anything about what they had done in the group so far. Between my stomach and the hockey group, I guess I had just been too pre-occupied to find out.

"It's really good," Al said. "The kids love the stories we read to them. They're learning to recognize more and more words every time."

Randy plucked a piece of pepperoni off her slice, blew on it, and then popped it in her mouth. "Yeah. The group is pretty big, so I do coloring and drawing with some kids while Al and Sabs read to the others. That way we have two smaller groups so everyone gets more attention."

"That makes a lot of sense," I said, holding a hand over my stomach.

"Oh, Katie! I forgot to tell you," Sabs said suddenly. "Mrs. Walker said it would be fine for our group to go to your scrimmage next Friday."

That was really good news, since Mrs. Walker had told us that a lot of the kids' parents would be working and wouldn't be able to attend the game.

"Katie, are you feeling all right?" Al asked,

changing the subject. "You haven't been eating very much lately."

"Yeah, Katie. You have been acting kind of out of it lately," Randy agreed.

Sabs stared at me with a concerned expression on her face. "You look kind of pale, too," she commented. "Ohmygosh, Katie, are you sick or something?"

Looking around the table, I noticed that everyone else was starting on their second slice. I looked down at the slice of pizza in front of me, with only one bite taken out of it, and I knew I couldn't lie to my friends anymore. I had to blink a few times to keep from crying.

"Actually, for the last couple of days I've had a stomachache," I admitted, trying not to make it sound like a big deal. I mean, I didn't want to blow this whole thing out of proportion.

"It's probably a stomach virus," Randy said with a knowing nod.

"Yeah, Luke's got it too. He says that half the high school is out with it," Sabs added. "Maybe Emily brought the virus home and gave it to you." She looked glad to think that it

54

wasn't anything terrible.

"Really?" I asked, feeling a big rush of relief. If a lot of other people had this stomach thing, then it definitely wasn't serious. "That must be what I have, too."

"Did your mother take you to the doctor?" Al asked as she wiped some pizza sauce from the sleeve of the blue cowboy shirt she was wearing.

I shook my head. "Not yet," I replied, without telling her that I hadn't even told Mom about my stomachache yet. "If it doesn't go away by next week, I'll definitely go see one."

"Well, I hope your stomach can handle *Invasion of the Body Snatchers*!" Randy joked, gulping down half of her glass of milk. Horror movies are one of Randy's favorite things in the whole world. We must have seen a million of them since we've gotten to be friends with her.

Sabrina's hazel eyes opened wide, and she exclaimed, "I don't know how I'm going to make it through four scary movies! I am definitely going to have to close my eyes for the gory parts."

I was glad that my stomach was forgotten

for the moment. And I was really glad that I wasn't the only one in the world with this bug.

If it was just a stomach virus, there was nothing major to worry about. Was there?

Chapter Six

Wednesday morning I sat alone at our large dining room table and forced myself to eat some oatmeal for breakfast before school. My virus was still going strong. Not only did I have a stomachache, I was also hot and cold at the same time, not to mention tired and dizzy.

It had been a whole week now since my stomach had started hurting. I would definitely tell Mom about it today, since it looked like it wasn't going to get better on its own.

I decided not to say anything until after I got home from the hockey league this afternoon, though. I knew Mom would insist that I skip the Acorn League today, but there was no way I was going to do that. Today was our last practice before the kids' first game on Friday, and I had to be there. I couldn't let these kids down, especially since a lot of their parents wouldn't be there to see them.

I was sipping some fresh-squeezed orange juice when Michel came striding into the dining room carrying his schoolbooks and looking excited. Luckily Michel never holds a grudge and he wasn't mad at me anymore for yelling at him Saturday morning.

"Great news, K.C.!" he said, straddling one of the antique dining room chairs and smiling at me. "I told Papa about the Acorn League and the kids. When he heard about the scrimmage Friday and how the kids don't even have matching shirts to play in, he said he was going to call the sporting goods store at the mall and have matching jerseys sent over for everyone! Isn't that great?" Michel finished breathlessly.

I nodded, feeling pretty excited myself, in spite of my stomach. "That's fantastic! Mrs. Walker will be really happy." Uniforms were just what the kids needed to boost their confidence for the scrimmage. They were all nervous about the game, even though it was informal and no one expected them to play like a professional team or anything.

"So, are you ready for school? I ate earlier,"

Michel said, getting up from the chair and heading for the foyer.

I pushed my half-eaten oatmeal away and nodded. I would definitely tell Mom about being sick right after practice today. Maybe the doctor could give me some medicine to make me feel better and get my appetite back. I hadn't eaten much at all lately, and my clothes were starting to get all baggy.

I looked up as Mrs. Smith came out of the kitchen, her coat and gloves already on. She was obviously ready to drive us to school, so I slowly got up and went to the foyer closet. I reached up to get my jacket off the hanger, but then I had to stop and lean my arm against the doorframe. Suddenly I felt very dizzy and flushed.

"K.C?" Michel asked, looking at me. "Are you okay? You're shivering and your face is all red."

I had to take a few deep breaths before I could trust myself to speak in a steady voice. "I think I just have the flu," I told him. "I'm going to tell Mom tonight. I'll go to the doctor tomorrow after school if they want me to."

Mrs. Smith was looking at me now, too.

"Maybe you should stay home from school today, Miss Katie. I could write you a note. I'm sure your mother would agree. I could call her at the bank and ask," she offered.

"No, I'm fine, really," I told her.

"If you say so, Katie," Mrs. Smith said in a concerned voice. "But if you are not feeling any better in school, call me right away and I'll come and pick you up."

"Thanks, Mrs. Smith. I'll call if I don't feel any better," I said.

Michel got my coat down for me and helped me on with it. For a brother, he really isn't too bad.

When we got to school, the halls were already crowded with students, so I pushed my way through to my locker. I glanced around but didn't see Sabs, Randy, or Al. They were probably at Randy's locker or something.

Everything looked kind of blurry, and my whole face felt hot. This virus was definitely getting worse. I squinted at the lock, fumbling with it until I got it open. The minute the door opened, an avalanche of Sabs's books fell out of the locker and landed at my feet.

I stared at them for a second and then let

out a long, slow breath. Sabs's half of our locker is always a complete mess. Usually I am pretty good at jumping out of the way, but today I just couldn't deal with it. The pain in my side got worse as I bent over to pick everything up. In fact, it was so bad that I had to grab onto the locker door to keep from falling over.

"Oops! Sorry, Katie," Sabrina said, walking up to our locker with Randy and Al. Sabs bent over to help me gather up her books.

I was feeling tired and angry and irritable, and suddenly all of those feelings just bubbled over. "Sorry! Is that all you can say, Sabs?" I cried angrily, struggling to stand up. "Why don't you just clean your half of the locker? I'm really tired of cleaning up after you all the time!"

Sabs's mouth fell open as she looked up at me, and her face turned from white to bright red. Next to her, Al and Randy were staring at me with shocked looks on their faces, too.

My whole body was shaking from my outburst. Grabbing my books for first class, I walked as quickly as I could down the hall, away from my friends. When I was around the corner, I stopped and leaned against a locker to catch my breath and steady myself.

I hugged my books close to me. Hot tears started to well up in my eyes, and I tried to blink them back.

"What's the matter with you?" I heard a totally unsympathetic voice say.

Oh, great, I thought to myself. Out of the hundreds of lockers in this school, I had picked Stacy Hansen's to lean on! She was standing right there, with her hands on her hips, looking at me as if I were some sort of science lab specimen or something.

I quickly wiped my eyes dry. "Nothing!" I snapped. I would have walked away right then, but I was suddenly so dizzy that I felt as if the hall was spinning in circles around me.

"Hah! Well, I don't know what you've got to be upset about. I mean, you live in a fancy house and you have tons of new clothes. You even managed to join that stupid hockey team for poor kids just so you can hang around Scottie twice a week!"

That was it. I just couldn't take Stacy anymore. "Why don't you stop talking about things you don't know anything about!" I cried. "I joined the Acorn League because those kids need help. If you ever thought about anything except yourself, you might see how important it is to help others, no matter how much or how little you have!"

The blood was pounding in my ears so loudly that I couldn't hear anything else. I turned around and was suddenly aware that a group of students had gathered around Stacy and me and was staring at us. They seemed really far away, somehow, as if I were looking at them through a long, hazy tunnel. Then the sea of faces swirled together and I felt myself falling.

I'm not really sure what happened after that. I never even felt myself hit the floor. The next thing I knew, I opened my eyes and was staring into someone's shirt collar. Moving my head, I saw that it was Scottie's and that he was actually carrying me in his arms!

"Scottie? What . . . " I wanted to tell him to put me down, but I felt really weak and woozy.

The next thing I knew we were going through the door of the nurse's office and Scottie was laying me down on the couch there. Everything was still kind of blurry, but I could see that he looked really angry and scared at the same time. I wondered if he was mad at me or something.

"Wh-what happened?" I managed to squeak out.

He knelt down next to me. "You were fighting with Stacy and then you just fainted," he said, still looking scared. "Luckily, I was there and I caught you."

Then Scottie hit the edge of the couch with his fist. "It's my fault!" he burst out. "I knew you were sick. I should never have believed you when you said you were fine!"

Suddenly the school nurse was bending over me and shoving a thermometer in my mouth. She hurried Scottie out of the office, closing the door right in his concerned face before I could even thank him for helping me or tell him not to feel bad.

I was still feeling dizzy and sweaty, and the pain in my stomach was worse than ever now. I guess I must have had a pretty high temperature, because when the nurse saw what it was, she drew in her breath sharply. She immediately started asking me all these questions about where I hurt and how long I had been sick. She sounded really urgent.

When I told her about my stomach, she gingerly pressed down on my abdomen. The shooting pain was so bad that I couldn't help crying out really loudly.

The next thing I knew, the nurse was calling an ambulance, and that made me totally panic. I was all alone, without my mom or my friends or anyone — and I thought I was going to die without ever seeing them again!

Chapter Seven

Sabrina calls Allison.

ALLISON: Hello?

SABRINA: Al, I don't know what to do! I've been calling Katie's house for an hour now, and there's no answer!

ALLISON: Did you try the main number or just Katie and Michel's line?

SABRINA: I tried every line. I even called information and got the number for Jean-Paul's office in the house. I'm so worried about Katie! I mean, she passed out right in the hallway and everything, and then the ambulance took her away. What if she's —

ALLISON: She's not! Calm down, Sabs. Scottie told us she was awake and talking in the nurse's office. I'm sure her family is with her at the hospital and that's why no one's home.

SABRINA: Well, I don't know why Mrs. Smith or the cook or anyone isn't answering the phone. I'm going to try again. I'll call you back later, okay?

ALLISON: Okay. Bye.

Sabrina calls Katie's line.

MICHEL: *Allô?*

SABRINA: Michel! Boy, am I ever glad you answered! Is Katie all right?

MICHEL: *Oui*, but she's really sick. She has to stay in the hospital until her fever goes down enough so they can operate.

SABRINA: Operate! Ohmygosh! What's wrong?

MICHEL: It's her appendix. The doctor says she has to have it out as soon as possible, by tomorrow morning, I think. I'm here packing some things for her. I don't have any idea what to bring, Sabrina. Can you help me out?

SABRINA: No problem. You should take a

nightgown and her robe and slippers. And probably a pair of sweatpants and a sweatshirt to come home in. And some underwear and a hairbrush!

MICHEL: But how can I find everything? I don't even know where she keeps things! I can't do this — I just want to get back to the hospital!

SABRINA: Michel, you sound really worried. Katie is going to be okay, isn't she?

MICHEL: The doctor says she will unless . . .

SABRINA: Unless what?

MICHEL: Well, unless her appendix bursts. He said it's been infected for about a week now. Oh—Mrs. Smith just came in to help me pack. I have to go.

SABRINA: Don't forget her toothbrush. And tell her we love her!

MICHEL: I will. *Au revoir*.

SABRINA: Bye.

Scottie calls Michel.

MICHEL: *Allô!*

SCOTTIE: Hi, Michel. How's Katie? I tried all day to get the nurse to tell me, but she wouldn't. Is Katie there? Is she okay?

MICHEL: Is that you, Scottie? She's in the hospital. She has appendicitis.

SCOTTIE: Wow, that's really serious. I knew something was wrong with her stomach. I mean, last week at hockey practice she practically fell over. I should have made her tell me what was wrong.

MICHEL: Don't feel bad. She didn't tell anybody she was so sick. The doctor said if she hadn't passed out and the nurse hadn't sent her right to the hospital, her appendix might have burst, and then it's really bad.

SCOTTIE: She's so stubborn! Why didn't she tell us?

MICHEL: Well, you know Katie. Listen, I've got to get back to the hospital now. Mom and Dad and Emily are there now.

SCOTTIE: Um, do you think I could . . . I mean, would Katie mind if I, uh, came to visit her for a minute?

MICHEL: Don't bother coming today. The doctor gave her so much medicine to get her fever down that all she does is sleep. They will probably operate first thing tomorrow morning. Maybe you should wait until Friday to go see her.

SCOTTIE: Okay, but you'll call me and tell me if there's anything up, right?

MICHEL: Sure. Oh, did you go to the Acorn League practice today? I hope Mrs. Walker wasn't mad, but there was no way I could leave the hospital. Mom is a wreck about Katie.

SCOTTIE: Everything's cool with that. Mrs. Walker said she understands and not to worry about the scrimmage. John and Dave and I took over today, and it went fine. (*He pauses.*) There is one thing, though. You know that little boy Katie likes so much?

MICHEL: You mean Danny?

SCOTTIE: Yeah. He was pretty upset that she wasn't there. He said something like he knew he couldn't count on anybody to keep their word, and Katie was just like his parents and didn't keep her promises. He even hit the other center over the head with his hockey stick. Do you know what that's all about?

MICHEL: No, and Katie is too out of it for me to ask her. But I'll definitely be there Friday for the scrimmage — as long as everything goes all right with Katie, I mean. I better go now, Scottie.

SCOTTIE: Okay. Don't forget to call me.

MICHEL: I won't. *Au revoir.*

Allison calls Sabrina.

SAM: Hello?

ALLISON: Hi, Sam. It's Allison. Did Sabrina find out anything about Katie?

SAM: Yeah, she did, but Mom called us for dinner right after she got off the phone with Michel, so she didn't have time to call you guys. She's really worried about Katie. She didn't even eat her spaghetti.

ALLISON: Oh, I'm sorry. Are you guys done eating? I don't want to interrupt. It's just that I'm really worried.

SAM: No sweat, we're done. Here's Blabs.

SABRINA: Sorry I didn't call, Al.

ALLISON: That's okay. Sam said you talked to Michel. What did he say?

SABRINA: Katie has appendicitis.

ALLISON: That's serious!

SABRINA: I know. Michel says her fever is really high and they have to remove her appendix before it bursts.

ALLISON: Oh, no!

SABRINA: I feel terrible, Al! I mean, Katie said at the sleepover that her stomach hurt, and I just told her it was probably a stomach virus! If anything happens to her, it's partly my fault. I can't believe I didn't take it more seriously!

ALLISON: I know what you mean. But you can't blame yourself, Sabs. Katie didn't let on at all that it was so serious, so there was no way we could know. And she did promise to go to a doctor if she didn't get better.

SABRINA: I guess you're right. This is really intense. I don't know how I'll be able to go to school tomorrow knowing that Katie is probably on the operating table.

ALLISON: That's how I feel, too. I haven't even been able to start writing my book report for English because all I can think about is Katie. Listen, I'm going to get off now and call Randy. I'm sure she'll want to know what's going on. I'll see you tomorrow morning.

SABRINA: Right. Bye, Al.

ALLISON: Good-bye.

Allison calls Randy.

RANDY: Yo!

ALLISON: Randy, I just found out from Sabs that Katie has appendicitis! She's in the hospital, and she has to get operated on tomorrow morning.

RANDY: Seriously? Is she going to be okay?

ALLISON: I think so. Unless it bursts, anyway. That can be really dangerous. I wish we could call her, but they won't let her have a phone in her room until after the operation.

RANDY: Hey, I have an idea! Why don't we make a card for her and all sign it? Then she'll know that we've been thinking of her even though we can't talk to her now.

ALLISON: That's a really good idea. Maybe we could even have the kids from school sign it. And everyone from the Acorn League, too.

RANDY: Cool! I'll make a really big one. I think my mom has a big piece of poster board, so I can start working on it tonight.

ALLISON: I'll help you with it tomorrow

	during lunch, too.
RANDY:	Okay. That will give us something to do besides worry about Katie. Tomorrow at school is going to be a drag. I wish we could just not go, and stay at the hospital all day instead.
ALLISON:	Well, we can call during our free periods and see if there's any news.
RANDY:	Okay. Well, I'd better get started on this card. See you tomorrow!
ALLISON:	Okay. Good-bye, Randy.

Chapter Eight

My whole body felt heavy and tired as I looked through blurry eyes at the walls of the hospital room.

It was still Wednesday evening, or at least, I thought it was. I wasn't really sure, because when I first got to the hospital, the doctor had given me medicine that had made me really sleepy. I figured it was evening, anyway, since I could see through the half-closed blinds in my hospital room that it was dark out.

The room was empty except for my bed, a chair, a TV hung high on the wall, and a small table next to my bed with a phone on it. Looking around it, I wondered where Mom was. I kind of remembered opening my eyes before and seeing her sitting in the chair, but maybe it was just a dream.

As I shifted to sit up a little, I felt a pinching

sensation in my arm. Glancing down, I saw that there was a needle in my left arm. It led to a soft bag half-filled with clear liquid that was hanging from a metal hook above my head. I wrinkled my nose and looked away.

Yuck! I didn't like the idea of the I.V. being stuck in my arm at all. I would definitely have to try not to look at it again.

I forgot all about the I.V. a second later, when I heard Mom's muffled voice coming from outside my room. "Dr. Stone, when will you be able to operate?" she asked.

I thought Mom sounded really worried, and then I heard Jean-Paul's voice say something, so I knew he had to be out there, too.

I strained my ears to listen for the doctor's answer. When I had first gotten here, Dr. Stone had told me that I would have to have my appendix removed, but I hadn't heard anything else about the operation. At least my stomach had stopped hurting because of the shot she had given me. Maybe that was a good sign.

I frowned and leaned a little closer to the door. The doctor was speaking so softly that I couldn't make out much of anything. Her monotone, technical-sounding voice came through the door in bits and pieces.

". . . the infection . . . a rupture could cause peritonitis . . . fatal . . . immediate surgery in most acute cases . . . wait until Katie's fever breaks . . ."

I hadn't heard all of what she said, but one word stood out in my mind: *fatal*! My heart started to beat fast as I fumbled for the nurse call button on the wall next to my bed. I wanted to call for Mom, but my throat had gone suddenly dry and I didn't think I could yell loudly enough for her to hear me.

It seemed like forever before a tall, slim nurse came into the room. I could still hear Jean-Paul and my mom talking to the doctor outside in the hallway.

"Good, you're awake!" the nurse said with a smile. She immediately put a thermometer in my mouth. I was used to this by now, since they had been taking my temperature every couple of hours for the whole day. I just wished that she had waited a second, because I really wanted to tell her that I needed to talk to the doctor, or at least Mom. I had to know what they were talking about!

Finally the nurse took the thermometer out of my mouth. She read it quickly, smiled, and told me, "Very good." She was back out the door before I could ask her anything.

I sat there staring at the empty doorway. I guess everything that was happening caught up with me then. Tears welled up in my eyes and poured down my cheeks.

"K.C.! *Mon Dieu*, don't cry! Everything will be fine!"

I blinked as Michel appeared in the doorway, carrying an overnight bag. He rushed over to me and sat on the edge of the bed, holding my hand. Emily was right behind him. She came over to my other side and gently pushed a stray strand of hair out of my face. "It's going to be all right," she said softly. "I promise!"

"But the doctor said it's . . . fatal!" I sobbed.

"No, she didn't!" Emily said right away. "Were you listening at the door?" she asked, shaking a finger at me.

I nodded, moving the arm that wasn't connected to the I.V. so I could wipe my eyes.

Emily took a deep breath. "What she said is that in some severe cases, if the appendix bursts and the infection spreads through the abdomen and it's not operated on immediately, it could cause peritonitis, which in some cases can be fatal. But you don't have to worry about that," she concluded quickly.

"That's right," Michel added cheerfully. "Dr. Stone is going to operate as soon as your fever goes down some more. Now that you're in the hospital, nothing bad can happen!"

I glanced at Emily. "Dad was in the hospital when he died," I whispered.

Emily's eyes started filling up with tears then, too. "I know. I keep thinking about that," she said softly. "But this isn't the same thing at all, Katie. You're not going to die. The doctor is absolutely certain about that."

"When is Mom coming in?" I asked. I really wanted to see her.

"I'll go get her," Michel offered quickly. He hopped off the bed and was out the door in a flash. I guess it was a little uncomfortable for him to hear us talking about our dad, now that Mom is married to Jean-Paul and everything.

Emily smiled at me, and I could tell she was trying to be cheerful for my sake. "Mom has been completely possessed all day," she told me. "She drove over here so fast from the bank that she got pulled over for speeding. And then she actually got the policemen to give her an escort to the hospital!"

I had to smile, picturing Mom ordering the police around like that.

"She and Jean-Paul are really worried, Katie," Emily went on more seriously. "Do you know they flew Dr. Stone in by helicopter from Minneapolis? She's supposed to be the best abdominal specialist in the Midwest."

Suddenly that awful terrified feeling started to come back. "Am I that bad? Is it really that serious?" I asked.

"No, not at all! You're going to be fine," Emily said quickly. "The doctor said appendicitis is actually very common. I guess Mom just doesn't want to take any chances."

Even though Emily didn't say so, I could tell that she was thinking about Dad again. Mom had pretended to be strong while he was in the hospital and even after he died, but I knew that inside it had almost destroyed her.

I looked up as Michel came back into the hospital room with Mom, Jean-Paul, and Dr. Stone. Mom came right over to me and kissed me on the forehead. She looked really worried and tired.

"Hello, Katie. You're looking better!" Dr. Stone said cheerfully. She was really tall and pretty, with dark hair and kind brown eyes. She looked just like all those doctors on hospital TV series — the kind with a face you can really trust. Somehow that made me feel a lot better.

"Dr. Stone, do you think you could operate now? I feel much better," I asked as she reached over and felt for the pulse in my wrist, keeping her eyes on her watch. I couldn't get that word *peritonitis* out of my mind. I wanted this appendix out of me before it burst!

Dr. Stone smiled. "Well, you're looking better, and the nurse tells me your fever's down some. But I think we'll wait until tomorrow morning. Your fever should be totally gone by then, and you could use the extra rest. You didn't do yourself any good by waiting so long to tell anyone you weren't feeling well, young lady!" she reprimanded gently.

I lowered my eyes. "I know. I'm sorry."

"Doctor, do you think I could sleep here tonight?" Mom asked.

I looked expectantly at Dr. Stone. I really hoped she would let Mom stay with me. I guess it was pretty selfish of me. I mean, Mom looked so tired and I knew she should go home. But I really didn't want to spend the night alone in the hospital.

My spirits lifted a little when Dr. Stone nodded. "Sure. I'll try to get a couch brought in," she told us.

Jean-Paul put his arm around Mom and thanked the doctor for all she had done for us.

"Oh, think nothing of it. You should be thanking the school nurse, who had the good sense to send Katie right to the hospital," Dr. Stone said. She nodded to us all, then let herself out the door.

"We should thank Scottie, too," Michel added after the doctor was gone. "He's the one who carried Katie all the way to the nurse's office after she passed out, and that's no small feat, eh?" he kidded, raising his eyebrows at me.

Hearing Scottie's name made me remember something. "Ohmygosh! The Acorn League!" I cried. "I missed practice today! And what about the scrimmage Friday?"

Emily looked at me as if I had lost my mind. "Katie, you can't be serious," she said.

"I don't think you'll be going to any practices for a while, Katie," Jean-Paul added sternly.

"Definitely not!" Mom agreed.

From the determined looks on their faces, I knew there was no way I could change their minds. I looked down at my hands, feeling really terrible about letting the kids in the Acorn League down.

"Let's go see about that couch, *ma chérie*," Jean-Paul said to my mom. Mom gave my hand a squeeze, and then she and Jean-Paul went back out into the hall.

"Don't worry about the league," Michel told me, sitting down on the bed again. "Scottie called before, and he said that Mrs. Walker understands, and that Scottie, Dave, and John handled the practice fine without us today."

I stared at Michel in dismay. "You mean, you didn't go to practice either?" I cried.

"Of course not! I had to make sure you were all right," Michel said. He looked hurt that I would want him to be at practice instead of with me.

"I promised Danny I would be there for him," I mumbled, more to myself than to anyone else. "First his mother couldn't come to Friday's game, and now I won't be able to go, either. Danny is going to hate me!"

Michel hesitated for a moment and then said, "I'm sure he understands. Besides, I'm going to be at the game Friday, and I'll explain how much you wanted to be there."

I knew I should be grateful that Michel was trying to help, but somehow I didn't think it would be enough. Danny was going to be disappointed if I wasn't there Friday, no matter how good a reason I had. And that made me feel really terrible. Of all the times to get appendicitis, this was definitely the worst!

Letting out a huge sigh of frustration, I cried, "Darn this appendix!"

Chapter Nine

"Katie? Katie?"

The voice sounded fuzzy and very far away. Then I woke up enough to realize that someone was really talking to me. I was floating in a woozy black fog, but I knew that I should answer the voice.

I tried to speak, but when I opened my mouth, all that came out was a moan. My lips and mouth were so dry that I could barely open them, and my eyes felt as if they were glued shut.

Finally I managed to open my eyes, only to see a blurry mess of lights and whiteness.

"Katie, this is Dr. Stone," the same voice spoke up again. "You came through the operation fine, and you're in the recovery room. Soon we'll be bringing you down to your room."

I blinked a few times until I finally focused

on Dr. Stone's face smiling down at me. Then the meaning of what she had just said sank in — I was fine! I didn't die!

I felt hot tears well up in my eyes, and then I heard myself say, "Mom." It came out kind of like a croak, but I guess she understood me.

"Your mother's waiting very anxiously for you in your room, Katie. You'll see her in a minute," Dr. Stone told me. She patted my arm and then walked out of the recovery room.

The next thing I knew, I was being pushed down the hall by two men in greenish uniforms. I figured I must still be on the rolling metal gurney they had used to bring me to the operating room early that morning. The overhead lights in the hallway whizzed past my eyes, and the motion made my stomach do flip-flops.

I felt as if I might be sick, so I closed my eyes for just a second to block out the lights. When I opened them again, I was in my hospital bed and Mom was sitting on a chair next to me.

"Hello, sleepyhead!" she said, smiling at me. She looked really happy to see me.

I had no idea how I had gotten from the

whizzing table to my bed. Had I fallen asleep? What time was it?

"Mom?" I said, swallowing to moisten my dry throat. I thought this operation was supposed to make my stomach feel better, but I was still very queasy. My stomach was hurting again, too, but I guess that wasn't surprising, since they had cut me open to take out my appendix. "I don't feel very well," I admitted.

"The doctor said the anesthesia might make you nauseous," Mom told me, nodding sympathetically. "Here, you can't eat for a while, so just take a sip of water."

I started to reach for the cup with my left hand, until I realized that the intravenous tube was still attached to that arm. I didn't want to take any chances of it falling out, so I dropped that hand and took the cup with my right hand instead.

Whatever they put me to sleep with before the operation must have been pretty strong, because I was having a little trouble making my hand work right. Finally I put the straw in my mouth, but my mouth was so dry that my tongue felt like dust. It hurt to swallow, but I forced myself to drink the water anyway. I guess it did make my stomach feel a little better. I was beginning to feel a little hungry, too.

"What time is it?" I asked, glancing around the room to find a clock. I didn't see one, but I did see some brightly colored cards and a vase full of flowers. I wondered who they were from, but I felt too tired to ask.

"It's about four o'clock in the afternoon. You slept for a while after the operation, but the doctor said it's good for you to rest," Mom explained.

Almost the whole day had gone by without my even knowing it. At least, I hoped it was only one day. "What day is it?" I asked hesitantly.

Mom smiled. "It's Thursday, honey."

I breathed a sigh of relief. At least I hadn't slept through the Acorn League's first game. That wasn't until tomorrow. Now that the operation was over, I was really hoping that I would be allowed to go to the game. Maybe Mom and the doctor would let me if I promised just to watch, not to coach or do anything active.

"Your brother and sister will be here any minute now," Mom went on. "I told Sabrina, Allison, and Randy that you couldn't have any other visitors until tomorrow. They called three times already today to see how you were. They all send their love and hope you feel better."

Knowing that my friends had called to see how I was made me feel really good. Right now, I would have given anything to see them. But I remembered how mean I had been to Sabs about our locker right before I passed out. I wished she were right there so I could apologize to her for that.

"When can I get out?" I asked. I was barely whispering, but Mom seemed to hear me. It kind of hurt my stomach to try to talk, but I had so many questions.

"Well, dear. You'll have to ask Dr. Stone that. Let me see if I can find her," Mom said. She got up from the chair next to my bed and slipped out of the room.

Luckily I didn't have to wait too long before Mom came back with Dr. Stone. I made sure that the first question I asked was when I could eat.

"Well, we'll try you on soft foods, Katie. If you can keep them down then that will be a good sign," Dr. Stone told me. I didn't know what soft foods were and I didn't know why if

I kept them down it would be a good sign, but I would be happy to finally get something besides water.

Then I asked the next most important question on my mind. "When can I go home?"

The doctor chuckled, her dark eyes twinkling. "That is another good sign! Well, in most routine appendectomy cases, the patient is released in three days."

I counted quickly in my head. I had gotten here yesterday, which was Wednesday. So tomorrow would be my third day here. "Tomorrow?" I asked hopefully, still thinking about the Acorn League scrimmage.

"No, Katie. Three days from the operation. I would bet, first thing Sunday morning," Dr. Stone said. I guess she saw the disappointed look on my face, because she added, "Maybe Saturday night if you're a very good patient and do everything I tell you. And that includes eating all your food and getting lots of rest."

She was being really nice, so I nodded and smiled. I mean, I didn't want her to think I wasn't grateful, since she had probably saved my life! But deep down I felt really bummed out about missing the scrimmage and letting down all the kids.

Somehow I knew I couldn't talk about that to Mom or Dr. Stone or anyone, though. I mean, they were worried about me, not about a bunch of little kids who were learning to play hockey. I just knew that there was no way they would understand how I felt.

Chapter Ten

I never realized how hard it was to do absolutely nothing. But Friday and Saturday, I found out!

For one thing, I woke up very early on Friday. When the nurse came in to give me my medicine, she said it was five forty-five in the morning. I guess it wasn't surprising that I woke up early, since I had slept practically the entire day before.

My side still hurt, but not nearly as much as before the operation. Matter of fact, I felt almost good. I certainly felt rested, which was more than I could say for Mom. She was already up when I awoke, but there were circles under her eyes, and she looked rumpled from sleeping on the couch the hospital orderlies had put in my room for her.

I don't know how I did it, but I finally convinced her to go home and get some more sleep. Mom even said she might go in to work for a few hours. I knew she had lots of responsibility at the bank, and she had already missed almost two days of work. If she missed a third day, too, I was afraid things there would really get messed up.

After she left, I kept busy for a little while by reading the get-well cards in my room. One was from my grandparents, and another from my aunt Elizabeth and uncle Ted. A card in the flowers said that they were from Jean-Paul. There was even a card from the nurse at school, which I thought was really nice.

There wasn't much to do after I finished looking at the cards. Everyone had been so worried about my appendix that I guess they hadn't thought about bringing me something to read or puzzles to do. I would even have been happy to do homework!

At least my room had a television. I used the remote to flick through the stations, but the hospital didn't have cable TV and there was nothing on the regular channels but talk shows and boring soap operas. The nurse came in every few hours to take my temperature and give me medicine. That broke up the day a little, but by eleven o'clock, I thought I would go crazy from boredom! I guess being stuck in a small, plain room with nothing to do does that to a person.

Finally I decided to count how many hours and minutes it would be until my friends would be here to visit. Michel had told me that he, Sabs, Randy, and Allison would be over right after the scrimmage, so I figured they would get here by five o'clock.

When my lunch came, I couldn't believe it was only twelve-thirty. I still had four and a half hours before my friends would arrive. If I lived through lunch, that is. Now I know why hospitals always deliver food to you under those plastic covers — it's so you can't see it or you'd run away! I was still on soft foods, which was basically gelatin or pudding and eggs. Yuck! Thank goodness the doctor said I could eat regular food for dinner. Trouble was, after I saw my lunch I didn't know if I should be looking forward to dinner.

None of the food had any flavor to it, so I pretended it was good and ate it as fast as I could to get it over with. This made the nurse very happy. Little did she know that I was only eating so that the doctor would let me out of the hospital early!

Even though lunch wasn't very good, it made me kind of sleepy and I dozed off for a while. When I woke up, I was happy to see that it was already three o'clock. Now there were only about two more hours until my friends would get here from the hockey rink.

Every single minute of those two hours seemed to take a whole lifetime. I found some cartoons on TV and watched them until finally the door to my room swung open.

"Sabs!" I exclaimed as she came in, carrying a handful of balloons that barely fit through the doorway. Randy and Allison and Arizonna were behind her, carrying flowers and a giant handmade get-well card.

I couldn't help grinning. Right then I knew I had the best friends in the whole world. "I'm so happy to see you guys!" I told them.

"Hey, Katie, how's it going?" asked Arizonna with a smile. Then he handed me a bunch of flowers. "I thought you might need something to cheer up these weird rooms." I smiled back at Arizonna and we all laughed.

Arizonna had a way of cheering anyone up.

"How do you feel?" Sabs asked. Letting go of the balloons, she came running over to the bed and hugged me gingerly.

"I'm fine, Sabs. You don't have to be so delicate, you know. I won't break!" I laughed and hugged her back. My stomach hurt a little where the doctor had made the incision, but I didn't even care.

Randy came over and propped the huge card up on the night table. It was decorated with tons of drawings and pictures from magazines that had been cut up and pasted on in a collage. I thought it looked really cool.

"Boy, Katie, you really know how to make a scene, passing out in the middle of the hallway like that!" Randy teased me. "You're all the kids at school have talked about for three days!"

Allison nodded and added, "We're so glad you're all right!" She had grabbed the long strings of the balloons and was tying them to the end of my bed.

"You guys are the best," I said. Looking at the card and the balloons and everything, I started to get teary-eyed. I blinked furiously and said to Sabs, "I'm really sorry I yelled at you on Wednesday. I didn't mean what I said."

"I'm the one who should be sorry," Sabs said. "I mean, first of all, the locker is a mess. I promise that by the time you come back to school it will be as neat as a pin. Secondly, I should have known how serious your stomach thing was. We're best friends. I can't believe I told you not to worry about it."

I didn't want Sabs to feel bad about that. "Well, it's my own fault, since I kept it such a big secret," I told her. "So what did I miss these last three days?" I asked. I didn't really care what they told me, as long as they stayed and kept me company.

Sabs bounced up and down and said excitedly, "You won't believe it! Stacy actually pretended to pass out in gym class just to get attention."

"You should have seen her. She was so melodramatic about it! And then for the rest of the day, she had Eva carry her books for her," Randy added, rolling her eyes.

I couldn't believe it. Being sick for real was a total pain. It seemed really dumb that anyone would actually want to pretend they were sick just to get attention.

"But she got hers," Allison told me. "The nurse made her lie down in her office for half the day and she missed the school pep rally for the basketball team. She was really mad about that, but it was her own fault."

I laughed, imagining how mad Stacy must have been to have her plan backfire. "Did I miss a lot of work?" I asked.

"Not too much. Some of the teachers gave Michel home assignments for you in case you're going to be out of school for a while," Sabs told me. She gave me a worried look as she asked, "Are you?"

"I hope not. I've been going crazy just sitting here all day," I admitted. "Dr. Stone thinks I might be out of the hospital by tomorrow night."

"That would be cool," Randy said. "We figured you might be here for a while, so we stopped by the store on the way over and brought you some things to keep you busy while you're recuperating." She unzipped her knapsack and pulled out a stack of magazines.

I should have known my friends would bring exactly what I needed. "That's great!" I told them. "I haven't had a single thing to read."

Al plunked a paperback book down on top of the magazines. "I brought this from my house, too. I hope you like it." I saw it was a book in the *Chronicles of Narnia* series, which I know is one of Al's favorites.

"Thank you, Al. You guys are fantastic!" I said, feeling like I might cry again.

"You must have gone batty in here the last two days! They don't even have cable," Randy said in astonishment. She had picked up the remote and was flipping through the channels.

I nodded emphatically. "Tell me about it! I never knew there were so many talk shows on during the day. They're really a drag."

Reaching over, I picked up the gigantic card that my friends had brought. I really wanted to see what everyone had written in it.

"Ohmygosh!" I gasped when I spotted Mrs. Walker's signature. "What happened at the scrimmage? I don't believe I forgot to ask you guys sooner! Did everything go all right? Who won? Did any parents show up?" I asked in a big rush.

Sabs smacked herself in the forehead. "I knew I had something important to tell you!"

"What? Did something go wrong?" I asked anxiously. "Where's Michel and Scottie?" I suddenly remembered that Michel and Scottie were supposed to come here today, also.

Randy looked at Sabs and Allison. "Um, they're going to be here soon," she said vaguely. "The game was great," she added quickly. "The team that you and Michel and Scottie coach won, two to one."

"Great!" I said, smiling. "I wish I could have seen it." My friends looked at each other again, and I wondered what was up.

"A few parents showed up," Al added before I could ask her what they were being so secretive about. "Not all of them, but Mrs. Walker said that it was more than she had expected for a weekday."

"The little kids from our reading group loved watching the game. Now they all want to be hockey players when they grow up! They all signed your card, too, see?" Sabs said.

I quickly scanned the card for Danny's name. My spirits fell when I didn't see it. "That's really nice," I said softly.

I didn't feel like explaining why I was upset. I just felt so bad about letting Danny down after I had promised to be there for him. I was hoping he would forgive me, but since he hadn't even signed my card when all the other kids from the program had, he was probably mad at me.

The sound of someone knocking on the door broke into my thoughts. I looked over and saw Michel pop his head in. "I hope you feel like visitors!" he said, a big smile on his face.

When he came in, I saw that he was wearing the new hockey jersey that Jean-Paul had bought for the league. Scottie walked in behind him carrying presents.

"Aren't you going to congratulate the victors?" Scottie asked, smiling at me.

I was happy to see the guys, even though I kind of felt like an outsider, seeing Michel in uniform when I wasn't. "I helped coach that team as much as you did, you know," I said defensively, wagging a finger at them.

Scottie exchanged a fake insulted look with Michel, then they both started laughing. "I guess you must be feeling like your old self again, since you're fighting with me already!" Scottie teased me.

"It was an awesome game, Katie!" Michel put in.

Hearing that made me feel sad all over again that I had missed it. "I wish I could have seen it," I said again. I felt like a broken record, but I couldn't help it.

"You can! Here, open this," Arizonna said, handing me a small brown bag with a red bow stuck on it. "Sorry I couldn't wrap it better," he apologized.

I opened the bag curiously. When I saw a video cassette inside, I looked up and asked, "Is it . . . ?"

"A tape of the game!" Sabs finished excitedly. "Arizonna made it for you."

"With some direction from me," Randy added.

"Not!" Arizonna denied.

"Hey, that camera angle from ice level was my idea," Randy argued.

"Well, thank you both anyway," I told them, laughing. "I can't wait to go home and watch it."

Michel came over to my bedside and handed me a box neatly wrapped in silver foil. "Here, this is from my father," he said.

I tried to open it carefully, but I ended up just ripping off the paper. Inside was a hockey shirt that matched the one Michel was wearing. It was royal blue and had THE ACORN LEAGUE written on the front next to a small printed golden acorn. On the back, it said COACH KATIE in gold letters.

"The other team's jerseys are red and gold," Michel explained.

"Wow, this is great! I love it!" I cried, holding the shirt up.

Scottie nodded. "Yeah, the kids liked the jerseys, too. They played really well today, both teams," he told me. He took a step closer to the bed, and I noticed that he was holding a small white box with a blue bow on it.

"Um, here. This is for you," Scottie said gruffly, looking a little embarrassed.

I opened the box slowly and pulled out a little teddy bear. It was dressed in a hospital gown and holding a small banner that said GET WELL SOON on it.

I grinned at Scottie. "Thank you. I love it!" I told him. I wasn't sure what else to say. I mean,

I had never before gotten a present from a guy I liked.

"Oh, it's so cute!" Sabs exclaimed.

Michel and Arizonna looked at each other and started cracking up. "Oooh! It's soooo cute!" they chorused together, imitating Sabs's voice and elbowing Scottie in the side.

"Cut it out, you guys," Scottie said, batting the other guys' hands away. He was blushing a little, and I knew exactly how he felt. It was kind of embarrassing to have everyone tease us like that. But I liked the teddy bear a lot, and was really happy that he had gotten it for me.

Putting the stuffed bear on the pillow right next to me, I quickly tried to distract the guys from teasing Scottie. "Thank you, everybody, for everything!" I said.

"But wait, there's one more surprise," Michel said. "This one is from me, and let me tell you, it wasn't easy getting it here!"

I crinkled up my nose, wondering what it could be. I had already opened all the presents my friends had brought in with them. Sabs, Al, and Randy looked at each other, then glanced expectantly at the door to my room.

"What?!" I asked, looking at them suspiciously. "You guys are hiding something. What is it?"

Michel opened the door and stuck his head back out into the hall. A second later, in walked Danny, wearing his blue Acorn League jersey and carrying a bunch of pink carnations in his hand.

My eyes got all misty as he handed them to me and said, "Here!"

"Thanks!" I said, giving him a big smile. Then I swallowed hard and said, "I'm so sorry I couldn't be at the game today, like I promised."

Danny shrugged. "No problem. We won anyway. Besides, you're going to be okay now, right?"

He was trying to act as if it was no big deal, but the look in his eyes told me he was happy to see me.

"I'm fine, Danny," I told him.

"Good," he said, nodding. "I have to go now. Mrs. Walker is waiting outside in the van with the other kids. Bye!" And then he was gone.

He hadn't said much, but I didn't care. He had come to visit me, so maybe I had made a difference in his life. And knowing that made me feel on top of the world.

Chapter Eleven

"Hey, Coach Katie!" I heard Randy yell from the stands at Bradley Junior High's hockey rink.

I turned and saw Randy, Al, and Sabs sitting with the rest of the kids from the Acorn League reading group. I waved at them and did a figure eight on the ice.

It felt great to be back on the ice! I had been out of the hospital for exactly six weeks now, and my mother had finally agreed to let me coach the Acorn League again. I was really glad, since that meant I could help out with today's big game, which was the second time parents were invited.

The kids from both teams were lacing up their skates and warming up on the ice. I watched them, skating slowly around the edge of the rink. They were really pretty good now as they whizzed around in their red and blue jerseys, passing the puck in practice.

"Katie!" Mrs. Walker waved to me from across the rink. I waved back and skated over to her.

"Katie, I just have to tell you how much you and your family have helped the league and these children," she told me when I reached her. "The uniforms make such a difference. The kids feel really professional now, and even some of their friends from back home want to join. It looks like we're going to have four teams by next year."

I would definitely have to tell Jean-Paul this. I knew he'd be as happy to hear it as I was.

"And what Michel did while you were sick!" Mrs. Walker continued with a fond smile. "It's just amazing!"

I looked at her, feeling confused. "I don't understand," I said. "What did Michel do?"

Mrs. Walker looked at me in surprise. "You mean, he didn't tell you?" I shook my head. "Well, Danny was very upset when you didn't show up for practice before the first exhibition game. He even said he was going to quit the team."

"No!" I gasped, feeling terrible. This was exactly what I had been afraid of. Why hadn't anyone told me?

"But Michel went all the way over to his house to explain to him why you couldn't make the scrimmage," Mrs. Walker went on to explain. "Danny was pretty upset about it at first, but after Michel talked to him, he agreed to keep playing hockey. Now Danny seems like a completely different boy from the rebellious kid who first joined. I knew that what all these kids needed was someone to really care about them." Mrs. Walker looked at me with a smile as she finished.

This was a total surprise. And Michel had never said a single word to me about it! I guess he just didn't want me to worry about it when I was so sick and all.

"Well, thank you for giving us the opportunity to help, Mrs. Walker. It means a lot to us, too," I said sincerely. "I better get back to the warm-ups. We want to be all ready for our second exhibition game!" With a wave I skated back onto the ice.

I saw that Scottie was just finishing helping Joanna lace up her skates. Skating over to him, I asked, "Is everybody ready?"

"Almost," Scottie said. He was just getting up off his knee when I felt something painful under my toe.

"Ow!" I cried, bending over and grabbing my skate at the toe.

Scottie practically leaped to my side. "Katie! What's wrong? Are you all right? Is it your stomach?" he cried.

I stood back up and tried not to laugh. "I'm fine. I've just got a rock or something in my skate. Relax, Scottie. I've only got one appendix, and it's gone!" Then I couldn't help it — I burst out laughing.

"Sure, joke about it," Scottie said, looking annoyed and embarrassed at the same time. "You're just lucky I was there when you passed out!"

"I know. I thank you very much, Scottie," I told him. Then, before I even had time to think about what I was doing, I leaned over and gave him a peck on the cheek.

Scottie just stood there, looking at me in total shock. Suddenly I felt completely embarrassed that I had just done that.

"Um, I have to go see Danny," I said. I felt

my cheeks beginning to burn. Then I quickly turned and skated away.

It took me a couple of seconds to realize that I wasn't going anywhere near Danny. I took a deep breath to calm myself, then skated to the other side of the rink, where Danny was just stepping onto the ice.

"Hey, buddy! Are we ready to play?" I asked him.

"Yeah," Danny said, but he didn't seem at all enthusiastic. In fact, he looked almost as sullen as when I'd first met him.

"What's wrong?" I asked, looking him right in the eye.

Danny looked down, jabbing the blade of his skate into the ice. "I don't think my mom can make it again today," he finally mumbled. "I really thought she could, since it's Saturday. But then she said she had to work the morning shift at the diner and she might not be able to catch the bus here in time."

This wasn't great news, but I was glad that at least now Danny told me when things bothered him instead of pouting and being mean to the other kids, like he used to.

Glancing around, I noticed that quite a

few parents and brothers and sisters were already here to watch the game. "Oh, Danny. I'm sure she wants to be here," I began, trying to console him.

Just then I saw a petite, dark-haired woman wearing a waitress uniform walk in. She had wavy brown hair and big brown eyes, just like Danny. She was scanning the ice, looking at all the children. Then I saw her eyes light up when she looked at Danny, and I knew it was his mother. She had made it to the game after all!

"Hey, Danny," I said, ruffling his hair. "Do you know that lady who just came in?"

He turned around and immediately cried, "Mama!" In a flash he skated over to her and gave her such a big hug that he almost knocked her over.

I couldn't help smiling as I looked around to make sure the other kids were all ready. Both teams were out on the ice, so I skated over to the edge of the rink that was closest to where Sabs, Al, and Randy were sitting with the kids from the reading group.

My friends were totally surrounded by little boys and girls who were all clamoring for attention. Sabs's hair was a mess. Al was on one knee trying to pick up some crayons that one girl had knocked over, and Randy was giving a little boy a piggyback ride.

I felt so good inside that I smiled and called, "Hey, guys! Isn't this the best Saturday you ever had?" I knew it sounded corny, but it was exactly what I felt.

My friends all looked over at me and smiled back. All three nodded and said, "Definitely."

Don't Miss
Girl Talk #33
RANDY AND THE *PERFECT* BOY

"Randy? Are you with us?"

I quickly looked up to see Mr. Grey, my social studies teacher, standing over me with an amused expression on his face.

"Um, I agree with what you just said," I said quickly. Mr. Grey shook his head. "Nice try, Ms. Zak, but I'm not dumb enough to fall for that one. You weren't paying even the slightest attention, were you?"

"Well," I began, "I caught part of what you were saying."

"Which part?"

I shrugged and gave him my best grin. "The part where you said, 'Good afternoon, class.'"

That got a good laugh from the rest of the kids, and from Mr. Grey, too. For a teacher, he's pretty cool. Not to mention kind of cute.

"Well, if you can manage to stay with me for five minutes, I'll bring you up to date on what you missed," Mr. Grey said. "As you no doubt remember, a young man from Costa Rica named Rodolfo Ortiz is coming here for a month as part of a cultural-exchange program. He was supposed to stay with Michele Robinson's family, but her mother has suddenly become very ill. Now we have to find a new sponsor — a family who will let Rodolfo live with them for a month."

I nodded. "Got it, Mr. Grey. I'm with you now."

"Good." He grinned. "If you want, you can zone out again and I'll just update you in a few minutes."

But now I was actually interested in what he was saying. I had volunteered to have this Rodolfo guy stay with my mom and me. Four other families had volunteered, too, so Mr. Grey picked a name out of a hat to be fair. When Michele Robinson had been picked, I have to admit I was a little disappointed. Still and all, I thought it was cool that a kid from another country was coming to visit. I mean, Acorn Falls, Minnesota, isn't exactly the Excitement Capital of the World. We can use all the new and interesting people we can get.

TALK BACK!
TELL US WHAT YOU THINK ABOUT GIRL TALK BOOKS

Name _____

Address _____

City _____ State _____ Zip_____

Birthday _____ Mo._____ Year _____

Telephone Number (____)_____

1) Did you like this GIRL TALK book?

Check one: YES_____ NO_____

2) Would you buy another Girl Talk book?

Check one: YES_____ NO_____

If you like GIRL TALK books, please answer questions 3-5; otherwise go directly to question 6.

3) What do you like most about GIRL TALK books?

Check one: Characters_____ Situations_____
Telephone Talk_____Other_____

4) Who is your favorite GIRL TALK character?

Check one: Sabrina____ Katie_____ Randy_____
Allison_____ Stacy_____ Other (give name) _____

5) Who is your *least* favorite character?

_____

6) Where did you buy this GIRL TALK book?

Check one: Bookstore____Toy store____Discount store____
Grocery store___Supermarket___Other (give name)_____

Please turn over to continue survey.

7) How many GIRL TALK books have you read?
Check one: 0_____   1 to 2_____   3 to 4 _____   5 or more_____

8) In what type of store would you look for GIRL TALK books?
Bookstore_____Toy store_____Discount store_____
Grocery store_____Supermarket_____Other (give name)_____

9) Which type of store would you visit most often if you
wanted to buy a GIRL TALK book?
Check *only* one: Bookstore_____Toy store_____
Discount store_____Grocery store_____Supermarket_____
Other (give name)_____

10) How many books do you read in a month?
Check one: 0_____   1 to 2_____   3 to 4 _____   5 or more_____

11) Do you read any of these books?
Check those you have read:
The Baby-sitters Club_____   Nancy Drew_____
Pen Pals_____   Sweet Valley High _____
Sweet Valley Twins_____Gymnasts_____

12) Where do you shop most often to buy these books?
Check one: Bookstore_____Toy store_____
Discount store_____Grocery store_____Supermarket_____
Other (give name)_____

13) What other kinds of books do you read most often?
_____

14) What would you like to read more about in GIRL TALK?
_____
_____

Send completed form to :
GIRL TALK Survey, Western Publishing Company, Inc.
1220 Mound Avenue, Mail Station #85
Racine, Wisconsin 53404

**LOOK FOR THE AWESOME GIRL TALK BOOKS IN
A STORE NEAR YOU!**

Fiction
 #1 WELCOME TO JUNIOR HIGH!
 #2 FACE-OFF!
 #3 THE NEW YOU
 #4 REBEL, REBEL
 #5 IT'S ALL IN THE STARS
 #6 THE GHOST OF EAGLE MOUNTAIN
 #7 ODD COUPLE
 #8 STEALING THE SHOW
 #9 PEER PRESSURE
#10 FALLING IN LIKE
#11 MIXED FEELINGS
#12 DRUMMER GIRL
#13 THE WINNING TEAM
#14 EARTH ALERT!
#15 ON THE AIR
#16 HERE COMES THE BRIDE
#17 STAR QUALITY
#18 KEEPING THE BEAT
#19 FAMILY AFFAIR
#20 ROCKIN' CLASS TRIP
#21 BABY TALK
#22 PROBLEM DAD
#23 HOUSE PARTY
#24 COUSINS
#25 HORSE FEVER
#26 BEAUTY QUEENS
#27 PERFECT MATCH
#28 CENTER STAGE
#29 FAMILY RULES
#30 THE BOOKSHOP MYSTERY
#31 IT'S A SCREAM!
#32 KATIE'S CLOSE CALL
#33 RANDY AND THE *PERFECT* BOY

MORE GIRL TALK TITLES TO LOOK FOR

Nonfiction
ASK ALLIE 101 answers to your questions about boys, friends, family, and school!

YOUR PERSONALITY QUIZ Fun, easy quizzes to help you discover the real you!

BOYTALK: HOW TO TALK TO YOUR FAVORITE GUY